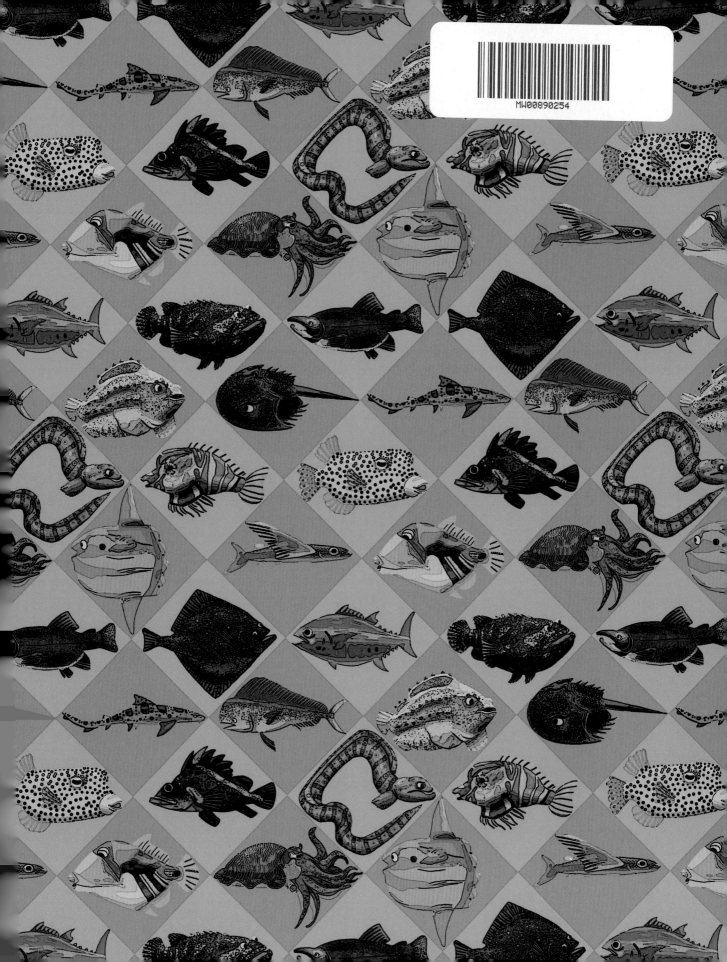

Oscar

A Frogfish's Guide to the Aquarium

by Rob Albanese

For M-. Thanks for all your love, support,
and encouragement throughout this process. You've
never stopped believing in me.

To my children: I hope you never stop exploring.
- RA

Frogfish Studios LLC
12345 Lake City Way #437
Seattle WA 98125

Published by Frogfish Studios LLC

ISBN 13: 978-1732502802
ISBN 10: 1732502803

I am Oscar Frogfish.
The aquarium is my home.
All the animals like each other,
no matter how strange we seem to some.

Clownfish is covered in snot-like slime
to avoid anemone stings,
but the reason he makes it his home
is for the food its tentacles bring.

INDO PACIFIC
CORAL REEF

In most species of
clownfish, the
male is the parent
who cares for the
eggs. He does
his by guarding
them from predators,
and he fans them with his fins
to help them develop..

FUN FACT:
Clownfish are
covered in slime to
protect them from
the sting of the
sea anemone.

Sea otter blows bubbles in her fur
to make a warm air coat.
This protects her from the cold
and also helps her float.

Sea turtle leaves her home
to travel far and wide.
She returns with turtle GPS
as good as your phone has inside.

French angelfish will stick together
through any ups or downs,
but they don't have room for other fish
or even like them around.

Salmon start their life in a stream
and then move on to the ocean.
Only when they're old and gray
do they return in slow motion.

Arapaima lives in murky water
which can be hard to leave,
so when he needs more oxygen,
he gulps it from the air to breathe.

The Amazon Basin

Moray eel has a second set of teeth
found inside his throat.
The teeth pull down his food
so he doesn't choke.

Pufferfish is usually flat
with her spikes all laid down.
But she can suck lots of water in
to blow up big and round.

Lionfish is striped
with white and red lines.
This tells other fish,
"Stay Away!" from my deadly spines.

Octopus has brains in her tentacles
and some might think this is great
But using her smart tentacles
she can only count to eight.

Tide pool sea stars and sea urchins
move around on tiny tube feet.
Urchin bites some rock to hide
while Sea Star uses his stomach to eat.

Whale shark eats tiny plankton
but grows larger than a bus,
and you'll never get so big as that
eating only french fries and chicken nuggets.

Grab a gift to remember us,
a plushy toy or two
because after your visit
we won't soon forget you.

I forgot to say how the frogfish do.
We are master spies
watching the world go by
while we put on our background disguise.